The 100 Patches of Hayward Stilton

REESE BETTLEYON

Archway Publishing books may be ordered through booksellers or by contacting:

Archway Publishing
1663 Liberty Drive
Bloomington, IN 47403
www.archwaypublishing.com
844-669-3957

ISBN: 978-1-6657-2268-1 (sc)
ISBN: 978-1-6657-2267-4 (hc)
ISBN: 978-1-6657-2266-7 (e)

Print information available on the last page.

Archway Publishing rev. date: 04/25/2022

Dedication:

I would like to dedicate this book to my third grade teacher, Mrs. Roberts, and to my loving family, for always supporting me and fueling my passion for writing.

Some say scarecrows can't do anything that people can. This story is about a normal scarecrow that proved this wrong.

A busy farm stretched out for miles and miles, with a field of wheat, corn, lettuce and pretty much every food you can imagine. In the midst of the wheat field, a tall scarecrow named Hayward Stilton stood, well, more like hung. A tall wood pole made of Redwood held the scarecrow by his arms, and quite often he pondered his purpose. If he was hanging there, with only the animals to keep him company, what was in his future? How long would his life go on like this? Would he ever be free?

One sunny day, a fox came prowling over. "What a fine hat that is, Hay!" he said in an awed tone.

"Why, it is, but I'd trade it for freedom if I got the chance. " he replied, looking longingly out at the fields of produce. "I want to go on an adventure, ya´ know, what if there is more out there, in the big world."

"And I thought it was crazy a bee could fly." A distant voice muttered, sounding awestruck. The scarecrow detected that the voice was coming from behind him. A chilly breeze made the scarecrow's baggy, plaid, pants ruffle and dance. "Who are you?" Hayward asked.

"Theodore the field mouse, thank you very much." the voice replied. Sure enough, a tiny field mouse loomed into view. He was brown and skinny, he had obviously been scrounging for food. *Poor thing! I wish I had some breadcrumbs for him!* Hayward thought. *I guess a scarecrow talking could be weird.*

At the sight of the fox, the mouse scurried off without another word, and off he ran into the endless fields skittishly, as the wheat glowed golden with the rising sun. "Well, I'd better be going, then." the fox said distractedly. "The farmer is on his last straw."

"Oh...okay...bye then." said the scarecrow, trying to look as if the corn stalks flowing in the wind interested him, when really, he was sad. Why was he sad, you ask Reader? He was *lonely*. He was so familiar with the farm, the rooster crowing, the cows mooing, the pigs snorting. He was content, but he had a strange thirst, a longingness of some sort, a *dream*. Would he ever get off his pole?

His thoughts were interrupted by a strange, deep, booming voice that echoed through the hills and mountains. "Hayward Stilton, right?"

All of the sudden...a human? A...walking tree? No, a... a *Scarecrow?* Yes indeed, it was Reader! He had a straw hat, a blue ribbon wrapped around it rippled in the wind as his long legs tramped through the field. He had baggy pants, almost see-through; the sun was shining, making the hay on the scarecrow glisten. He had a button-down plaid shirt. Hayward saw a grown, weathered version of himself. "Wha, what–" he began, but was soon interrupted.

"Silence! I cannot stay long, for I have places to be! By the way, I'm Old Thomas, the Scarecrow of Memories!" the older scarecrow half-shouted. "I have a task for you! See all the patches on my clothes?" Thomas gestured toward the patches that said names like *Anderson* or *Johnson.* "You will be getting these too, on a very important journey. You shall go to different families every year; and you shall henceforth be the Scarecrow of Thanksgiving!"

"Wow, ok!" Hayward said, and a strange sensation rushed through him, and the curiosity, the urge of freedom, was cured. "When do I start?" he asked, gazing at the older scarecrow's patches. It seems crazy, but, yes reader, he counted. 100 in all.

"Tomorrow night, be ready!"

"Yep! I've been waiting and waiting and–" he was once again interrupted.

"Silence! You shall not be greedy, for you bring good luck! Greediness ends up turning into problems!" Thomas exclaimed warningly.

"Ok! Hayward said again, curious, "Where is my first stop?"

"You'll see!" Thomas said with a polite cackle. *Heh heh!*

"Ok!" Hayward said for the third time.

"Well, see you then!" Thomas said, gesturing to a cornstalk.

"Huh?" questioned Hayward, perplexed.

"That is the portal that leads to the families. See, I am done going to different families, so I have a *permanent* home." Thomas said.

"Got it!" Hayward replied.

"See you later!" Thomas said.

Hayward waved, and thought about it all, thinking of all the families he would meet tomorrow night. *"I'm actually going to go and see what is going on in the world,"* He thought triumphantly. He thought all night, because, well reader, you know, scarecrows can't close their eyes, or move. Suddenly, a thought struck Hayward hard, he didn't know why he hadn't thought of it before. *How do I get off my pole?* He assured himself that Thomas would tell him. He cleared his mind and savored the last moments of night.

Soon the birds were chirping, the sun was rising, and Hayward had not even the slightest idea of how he was going to keep himself entertained. He managed the morning, where he filled the animals of the farm in on his coming adventure. They all gasped and cheered and chanted, *"Haywards gettin' patches, Haywards gettin' patches, Aren't 'ya Hay?"*

Hayward knew they were confused; the story was complicated.

"Yep! I am, meet'n families all around the world!"

BANG! BAM! CRASH! PHEWWWWWW!

All of a sudden sounds echoed through the fields, causing a ricochet effect to rotate around the farm. As you probably expected, the animals scurried away into the wheat, then through the stalks of ready-to-be-picked corn. The harvester rumbled past, groaning and crashing through the fields, and, as usual, Hayward froze. Once the tractor was out of sight and earshot, Hayward sighed. The afternoon sun crept over Hayward, and he was relieved to know that this time tomorrow, he would be... *Free*. He savored this thought, this feeling, of pure *Happiness*. As the scarecrow hung there on his pole, he listened to the animals whimpering and asking each other if they thought more sounds were coming. The sun slowly started sinking towards the horizon, leaving Hayward waiting for Thomas.

The moon came up, and the old scarecrow appeared.

"Ready?" he asked challengingly.

"Ready!" Hayward replied, ready for what was coming.

"Ok, 3...2...1!!!" Thomas said, with a flourish of his hand, making Hayward perplexed.

Just like that, Hayward was on his feet, off his pole, *on the ground!*

"Come on!" Thomas said impatiently.

"Oh, ok." Hayward said, though he was confused.

He took a step. He took another. Left, Right, Left. *He was walking!*

Thomas was in front of him, walking towards a cornstalk. To Hayward's surprise, he walked right through it!

"Come on!" Thomas's voice came from somewhere inside the stalk.

Hayward edged forward, stuck an arm through, and it disappeared! He took a deep breath and jumped through!

He spun and spun as bright colors swirled around him, until...

He was sitting on a hay bale, pumpkins surrounding him, on a big porch, and he had a view of a neighborhood, with houses big and small, this house in particular, was *big*. We're talking *crazy big*. A mansion! After about 15 minutes, a herd of kids came bursting out of the door, most looking hungry and wild. There were boys and girls, babies and toddlers, and even a frazzled looking grown-up trying to settle the kids down. "Ok! Time for dinner!" she called.

"No, I wanna see the scarecrow!" a little kid whined. "Us too, us too!" chorused the other children.

The kids hurried over and stared at Hayward like he was the most fascinating thing they had ever seen. Then the grown-up quickly herded the curious kids into the house.

About an hour later, the grown-ups led the mob of kids out to the porch. This time they were covered in food, looking wilder. The grown-ups stopped and stared at Hayward and asked if anyone knew where the scarecrow came from.

"We actually don't know!" one of them replied.

Later that evening, when the kids were sleeping, the grown-up's laughter could be heard from inside. Hayward loved the feeling that he was not alone. At midnight, when everyone was sleeping, Hayward heard a familiar voice.

"Well done, Hayward, well done!"

"Thomas!" Hayward whispered in shock.

"Yes, yes, it's me!" Thomas said loudly.

He winked when all of the sudden a patch appeared on the scarecrow's sleeve. Hayward gasped. It said...

The Hensens

And

The Petersons

"Told 'ya there would be patches!" Thomas said, laughing, "We are going forward in time!"

They were swirling again, this time they landed in a big city, and the same thing happened. He surprised a family and got a patch.

The Stanleys.

He then went to a house with a big backyard, and one with fancy flowers in the yard. He repeated this countless times, until he almost had 100 patches! He traveled to a farm, not different from the one he used to live in. On his last journey, he cheered up a lonely Grandma, whose kids were far away from her.

As the last patch appeared, Hayward smiled contently, and went swirling around back to the farm. It had not changed that much, except for a new scarecrow, on Hayward's pole! Hayward told him about the journey *he* would take. He tried to act like Thomas, he talked loudly, and acted fancy. Thomas was watching from behind one of the corn stalks, and he said, "A classic, it is, The 100 patches of Hayward Stilton!"

The scarecrow Hayward taught was named David, he did the same thing, and it went on for generations. It's still going now! Just look out your window, and maybe you'll get a special Thanksgiving surprise!

Printed in the United States
by Baker & Taylor Publisher Services